Disney

Herbie FULLY LOADED

OFFICIAL

MOVIE SCRAPBOOK

Text by Emma Harrison

Disney
PRESS
New York

When I graduated from college, I did not expect anyone to make a big deal out of it. As proud as my dad was of me, he has never been a balloons–and–streamers type of father. So when Dad told me he was going to buy me a car as a graduation gift, you could see the shock on my face from a mile away. Then he took me to Bumper Bonanza–basically a scrap heap in disguise–and told me I could pick whatever I wanted. Now there was the dad I knew and loved!

Little did I know that in that big pile of dented fenders and crushed windshields, I would find a car that would change my life. I know it sounds strange, but you would have to meet Herbie to understand. Yep. Herbie. That's my car. And he's not just any car. Herbie taught me what it means to be a friend, and how important it is to follow my dreams.

I've put this little scrapbook together so that Herbie and I will always remember our first adventure. So buckle up, sit back, and get ready for one wild ride!

Love,

Maggie

MAGGIE PEYTON

So here I am, a college graduate, and everything is turning out the way it's supposed to. I've landed a killer job as a production assistant at ESPN, my best friend Charisma and I are moving to New York together in a month, and my dad couldn't be happier.

I mean, I am, too, of course. Happy, that is. It's so cool, right? Charisma and I will be sharing an apartment, and doing the living-on-our-own, independent thing. And, well, even though I have no idea how I'm going to afford the first and last month's rent on my new apartment . . . and even though the very idea of taking a subway to work every day makes me cringe . . . and even though all I've ever really wanted to do was be part of Team Peyton . . . Wait, where was I going with this again? Right! New York. It's going to be great. Really.

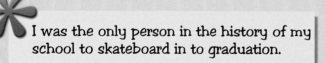

I was the only person in the history of my school to skateboard in to graduation.

Me and my dad.

The Peyton family trophy wall.

Age: *21*

Nicknames: **Sparkplug, Mag-Wheels**

Favorite place: **Behind the wheel of a race car**

Likes: **Junk food, working hard**

Dislikes: **Fake people, making my dad worry**

What everyone thinks I want:

To move to New York and start my new job at ESPN

What I really want:

To stay in Riverside and be a NASCAR driver, to win a major race

Stupidest moment of my life:

**Driving my car into a tree during a street race and ending up in the
hospital for two weeks**

Embarrassing secret: **Had a crush on Trip Murphy when I was thirteen**

Never seen without: **My skateboard**

RAY PEYTON, JR.

Ray is my big brother, and he's Team Peyton's current star driver in car #56. Well, "star" may be overstating it a little bit. Ray has never placed in the top ten in a race. Not once. It's not that he doesn't try. He's at the racetrack practically 24/7. I think he just doesn't have the racing gene. I know he would much rather be writing music and playing drums in his band. But, like me, Ray just wants Dad to be happy, and what makes Dad happy is having his son continue the Peyton legacy.

* Ray and his band. What a freak!

 He may not be the greatest driver, but he knows how to ham it up!

Age: *23*

Nickname: *In-the-Way Ray (because he's so slow he holds up the other drivers)*

Favorite place: *Sitting at his drum set*

Likes: *Rock music, writing songs, torturing his little sister*

Dislikes: *His nickname, the fact that he has never won a big race*

What everyone thinks he wants: *To be the next great Peyton in NASCAR*

What he really wants: *To be in a band full-time*

Embarrassing secret: *To chill out before a big race, he plays drums on the tire stacks in the garage.*

Never seen without: *His drumsticks—unless Dad is around*

RAY PEYTON, SR.

My dad at graduation— such the proud Papa.

Ray, Sr. is my father, the guy who runs Team Peyton. He and my grandpa were the original Peyton superstars. Dad misses racing, which is why he's so gung ho about Ray taking over. But I think he misses my mom even more. See, Mom died ten years ago, but when she was alive, she was my father's everything. Sometimes I think he sees her in me. That's probably why he was so upset when I got in the big tree accident. And why he doesn't want me racing now. Dad's dream is to see Team Peyton back on top. I just hope we all find a way to make that happen.

Dad finds Herbie at the junkyard.

Favorite place: *The racetrack*

Likes: *His team to win, but it's been a while*

Loves: *His kids*

Dislikes: *Dishonesty*

His worst fear: *Me getting into another accident*

Embarrassing secret: *He doesn't have a clue when a woman likes him. (See: Sally)*

Never seen without: *Family pictures in his wallet*

KEVIN MELTZER

Kevin was one of my best friends back in my street-racing days. After the accident, I promised my dad that all that was behind me, so I haven't seen Kevin or spoken to him since I went away to college. It was hard leaving my friends behind, but leaving Kevin was the worst. We just had so much fun together, and he was always there for me. Now he owns and runs a custom auto body shop and is totally famous around Riverside for his wicked restorations. I'm so proud of him. He's really living his dream!

The best mechanic in town!

Age: *22*

Nickname: *Kev*

Favorite place: *Under the hood of a car*

Likes: *Restoring cars, watching me race*

Dislikes: *Quitters*

Embarrassing secret: *I think maybe he has a little crush on me.*

Never seen without: *A grease stain some-where on his body*

Isn't he a cutie?

CHARISMA

Charisma is my best friend from college. If you saw us walking down the street together, you might not think that we're a "good fit," but there's a lot more to Charisma than meets the eye. Sure she's beautiful, wealthy, and gets basically everything she wants, but that doesn't mean she's shallow. Charisma is the exact opposite. She's supersmart (she graduated with not one, but two, physics degrees), she's a great listener, she's very supportive and loyal, and she's a huge romantic. If I'm the down-to-earth girl, Charisma is the dreamer. She's always reminding me that I can be whatever I want to be. I love that about her.

Behind that smile, there's a super-brain!

My girl is so stylish.

Age: *22*

Knows a lot about: *Shopping*

Knows nothing about: *Cars*

Likes: *Physics, travel, New York*

Dislikes: *When people don't follow their dreams*

Embarrassing secret: *She drives about as fast as a turtle.*

Never seen without: *Her charge card*

9

SALLY

Sally is the coolest. She loves racing, she's totally successful, and she's way pretty!

Sally is an executive at Bass Pro Shops and she's been in our lives for as long as I can remember. Bass Pro sponsors Team Peyton, and Sally is Dad's contact within the company. A business colleague, you might say. Except that business colleagues don't usually make dinner for you, reapply their lipstick whenever you're around, and look at you like you're the most perfect guy on Earth. Yep, Sally's got it bad for my dad. So bad that it's obvious to the entire world—except my thickheaded father!

Favorite place: *The racetrack*

Likes: *My dad. A lot.*

Dislikes: *The fact that my dad doesn't realize she likes him. A lot.*

Embarrassing secret: *Has been convincing her bosses to keep sponsoring Team Peyton—even though we haven't won any races in a while—just because she loves my dad and his family*

Never seen without: *Her cell phone for calls to the office*

THE HERNANDEZ BROTHERS

Ah, Miguel and Juan. What can I say about them? There's no gearhead magazine that they don't subscribe to. There is no hood that they have not looked under. There is no driver that they can't talk endlessly about. These two live for cars. They worship cars. They think that they know everything there is to know about racing and engines and track speeds and . . . need I go on? They're totally egotistical and look down on just about everyone. But let me tell you, if there's a rare part you need to find or a certain vintage car you're looking for, the Hernandez Brothers will find it for you. For a fee, of course.

Like: *Everything about cars*

Dislike: *Anything that's not about cars*

Embarrassing secret: *They spend every single weekend at car shows and races.*

(Well, it's not much of a secret.)

Never seen without: *Their posse*

Oh yeah. They're so cool.

TRIP MURPHY

Trip Murphy is "the man" on the NASCAR circuit. At least he is according to the fans. Those of us who know him know that he's just a cocky, conceited jerk. His face is everywhere—on T-shirts, water bottles, fanny packs—and he walks around like this is a good thing. Like overexposing himself until we all want to heave whenever we see him is a plus. Okay, maybe I'm being a little harsh. There is one good thing I can say about Trip. He's an awesome driver. Practically unbeatable. He does deserve to be a star for that. I just wish he could be a little more humble about it.

Nickname: *The Rock Star of NASCAR*

Likes: *Himself, the many products with his face on them*

Dislikes: *Losing*

His worst fear: *That he'll end up a washed-up old driver doing commercials for a weight-loss product*

Embarrassing Secret: *He sleeps with a Trip doll.*

Never seen without: *A couple of beautiful women on his arms*

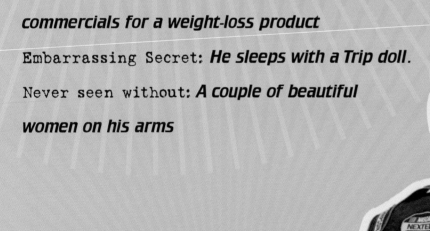

Classic Trip.

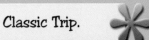

The World of Trip Murphy

FOR IMMEDIATE RELEASE

He's the number-one NASCAR driver in the world! He receives more fan mail in a day than any other driver does in a month! His face is more recognizable than Oprah Winfrey's!* And now, at the Trip Shop at Trip Murphy Racing, Inc. headquarters in downtown Riverside, you can purchase your very own piece of the Trip Murphy world!

We've got T-shirts, tank tops, leather jackets, and more, including the official #82 baseball cap worn here by Trip himself!

We've got steering wheel covers, driving gloves, and goggles. Even replicas of his #82 black, red, and yellow race car! Adorn your walls with Trip Murphy posters, photos, and the battery-operated Trip Murphy neon wall clock!

There's so much Trip Murphy stuff, we don't even have room to tell you about it all! Just come down to the Trip Shop at Trip Murphy headquarters and see for yourself!

(All major credit cards accepted; cash preferred)

• Coming soon: Driven, the official Trip Murphy aftershave AND a Trip Murphy video game that puts you in the driver's seat! Available for all major gaming systems!

*According to a recent poll of garage owners, mechanics, NASCAR ticket-holders, and members of the Trip Murphy fan club.

The Graduation Present

I couldn't have been more surprised when Dad took me to Bumper Bonanza to meet Crazy Dave and buy my graduation present. My very own ride! How lucky was I? Of course, when I saw the slim pickings at the junkyard, I wasn't sure what we were going to go home with. And then, I saw it. The perfect little white Nissan. I knew I had to have it!

Bumper Bonanza.
A real quality car lot.

It's a car pancake!

That is, until that other car fell on top of it.

So, seventy-five bucks later, there I was, the proud owner of a seriously banged-up hunk of metal.

What were we *thinking?*

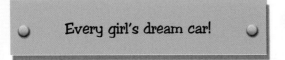

Every girl's dream car!

14

A Cryptic Message

After Dad did a little cosmetic surgery and handed over the keys, I decided it was time for me to get to know my new ride. I climbed inside and was just checking out the dusty old gauges, when the glove compartment suddenly popped open. Out fell an old, yellowing envelope with a handwritten note inside. This is what it said:

Please take care of Herbie. Whatever your problem, he'll help you find the answer.

Great! Apparently my new car was a fortune cookie in its former life. And Herbie? What kind of name is that?

The official passing of the keys.

The Shop

It was not my idea to go to Kevin's garage. I didn't even know he owned it! Herbie just sort of . . . took me there.

I hadn't seen Kevin in years. He was a little angry at first. Not that I could blame him. Herbie did almost flatten Kevin when he skidded into the garage!

I knew my dad wouldn't like the idea of Kevin and me hanging out again, but he offered to help fix up my new car. What was I supposed to do? Turn him down?

The Car Show

Kevin and I took Herbie for a test drive and Herbie totally took over! He was making turns when I wasn't touching the wheel. He was accelerating when my foot was nowhere near the gas pedal. Kevin, of course, didn't believe me. But by the time we got to the car show and Herbie finally stopped, I was ready to ditch him. I mean, this car could kill someone!

Kevin found this fire suit and helmet in the car. There was a name on the helmet: "Maxx." It was the perfect disguise.

Trip Murphy greets his public.

I didn't want to race Trip. I really didn't! But when Herbie gets his mind set on something . . .

We won! I couldn't believe it—neither could Trip!

HERBIE

Herbie is a car with a serious competitive streak, who never backs down from a challenge. In fact, he's often the challenger. He loves to race and he loves to win. He loves a lot of things, actually. He's got the biggest heart I've ever seen on a car. (Okay, the only heart I've ever seen on a car.) He also hates being insulted and will instantly let you know it—by squirting motor oil in your face or whacking you with a door or spraying you with windshield-washer fluid. Herbie is a true original, that's for sure. And he's full of surprises. You just never know what he's going to do next!

Nickname: *The Love Bug*

Favorite place: *Racing along the track*

Likes: *The thrill of the race, popping wheelies*

Dislikes: *Insults, scary movies*

Loves: *Sally's yellow car*

Embarrassing secret: *He's very emotional.*

Never seen without: *His number 53*

A Little Diagnostic Rundown

Things that work on my new car:

☐ **The horn**

Things that don't work on my new car:

- ◼ **Rear tires—they're not there**
- ◼ **Rear bumper—also not there**
- ◼ **Glove compartment—pops open of its own free will**
- ◼ **All the gauges**
- ◼ **The exhaust—it smokes**
- ◼ **The steering wheel—it jams**
- ◼ **The brakes**
- ◼ **The emergency brake—it comes off in your hand, which kind of defeats the purpose**
- ◼ **The shocks—can you say "ow!"**
- ◼ **The door springs—they keep popping open and hitting people**

Also—and no one believes this—the thing seems to have a mind of its own. . . .

I'm Not Going Crazy

By Maggie Peyton

I, Maggie Peyton, being of sound mind and body, do solemnly swear that my car did the following things today, totally on his own. (Maybe my family can use this document to get me out of the loony bin, which I am definitely headed for.)

1) Drove me to Kevin's shop and almost took his head off
2) Accelerated and popped a wheelie in the middle of a crowded intersection
3) Kept turning left no matter how hard I pulled the wheel to the right
4) Took us to the car show and stopped right in the middle of the action (I hit the brakes about ten times, but he didn't stop until <u>he</u> decided to.)
5) Honked his horn like crazy
6) Popped his own trunk
7) Squirted motor oil all over me
8) Slapped me into the car with his door (I SWEAR!)
9) Jerked to the right as I was passing Trip Murphy's car, leaving a huge gash in the perfect paint
10) Locked me in the car and Kevin out
11) Rolled up his own window
12) Sprayed Trip Murphy in the face with windshield-washer fluid
13) Took off in a race against Trip in front of thousands of people
14) Swiveled on his back bumper
15) Executed a killer rail slide
16) Beat Trip Murphy in an epic street race
    (Okay, well I maybe helped with that one a little!)

Herbie in Love

Aren't they just too cute?

I leave Herbie alone for one minute and all of a sudden he's smooching bumpers with Sally's little yellow car. I don't know why I'm surprised. Herbie's so emotional, of course he's a raving romantic. I think I see a few baby cars in our future. Although, I don't think that's biologically possible. But then, I didn't think a car with a mind of its own was possible either, so who knows?

The Car Show: The Fallout

Dad was not happy when he saw Herbie on ESPN, racing like crazy against Trip. I didn't want him to think I was street racing again and get all worried (after all, it was more Herbie than me), so I told him that Kevin's friend Maxx drove my car. I felt awful about lying, but I had to protect my dad. And besides, I wasn't going to do it again. Until we found that advertisement . . .

Herbie is trying to tell me he wants to race in Trip's Two-Day Racing Event.

THINK **YOU** CAN BEAT
TRIP MURPHY?
The Undefeated "Premier Series Champion"
THEN BRING IT ON!

TRIP MURPHY'S
SUDDEN DEATH SHOWDOWN

TWO-DAY RACING EVENT

$10,000 GRAND PRIZE

CAR SHOW • BURN OUT • SWIMSUIT CONTEST • SOUND COMPETITION

I knew it would break my father's heart if I raced again, but I needed that money for the security deposit on my apartment in New York. Without it, I wouldn't be able to take that job at ESPN, which was what my father really wanted.

So Kevin and I came up with a plan. We would enter Herbie in the race with Maxx as the driver. I would keep the helmet on, and no one would ever have to know that I was really Maxx. Now all we had to do was get Herbie ready for the race of his life!

Herbie in Training!

Getting Herbie in shape for the big race was a lot of work! Check out this page from my day planner that week.

WEDNESDAY THE 20TH

8 A.M.
Have a big breakfast. Lots to do today!
Pick up coffee on the way to the garage
(Note: Kevin likes high test!)
Stop by Jay's Auto Parts to check if
Herbie's new exhaust pipe is in
Get gas. Ultimate. Only the best for my Herbie.

8:30 A.M.
Go over Herbie's training plans with Kevin

9 A.M. - 12 P.M.
Engine overhaul
Add CO_2 tanks
Fit new timing belt
Change the oil to premium (Herbie deserves a good snack, too!)

12:30 P.M.
Replace tires

1 P.M.
Timed test drives

2 p.m.	Call Dad at the track to check on Ray's times
2:15 p.m.	Lunch! Something greasy and salty–followed by something chocolaty.
3:30 p.m.	Wash and wax
4:30 p.m.	Test new hydraulic system
5:30 p.m.	More timed test drives
7 p.m.	Home for dinner with Dad and Ray, hopefully with a good cover story for where I've been all day!
9 p.m.	Watch SportsCenter to see if they mention Trip and "Maxx"!!!

Herbie in Training!

Okay, so it may have been a ton of work, but we had a lot of fun, too. Kevin and I can have fun anywhere, doing almost anything. But when we're working on a car and speeding around the track and challenging ourselves? That's pretty much the best.

Behind the wheel is where I love to be!

Kevin takes his job as a trainer very seriously.

We had a blast together!

Herbie before . . .

. . . Herbie after!

Me as Maxx.

The New Herbie

Check out all of Herbie's improvements!

Waxed and buffed until gleaming.

Nitrious oxide tanks for serious speed (under the hood).

Shiny new bumpers.

Reflective rims.

New spoiler.

Brand-new, high-grip tires.

New hydraulic system and
shocks for a smooth ride.

Herbie

Trip Murphy's Sudden-death Showdown!

The two-day race basically worked like this: the first day dozens of drivers would take each other on in a series of elimination races. At the end of the day, the last drivers left standing would race one another. Whoever won that race would take on Trip Murphy the next day. If that driver beat Trip, he—or she—would win $10,000. It was a lot of racing, but Kevin, Herbie, and I knew we could do it. We had a great driver in . . . ahem . . . "Maxx." And we definitely had the best car!

Just a few of the cars Herbie and I had to take on that first day.

Trip and his lackeys kept an eye on us all day. You know they were freaking out as we left all our competitors in the dust!

Tomorrow it would be just Herbie and me against Trip and his state-of-the-art ride.

At the end of the day, Herbie was the only car left standing!

That night, Trip let me take his car for a spin! It was incredible!

Then we made a deal—tomorrow, we would race for pinks. That's pink slips—ownership papers. If Trip won, he would get Herbie. But if I won, which I knew I would, I would get to take home Trip's race car! Then my dad would have to take my dreams of being a NASCAR driver seriously!

The Final Showdown:
Trip Murphy vs. Maxx

The morning of the final race against Trip, Kevin told me that Herbie was acting a little funny. I was so nervous I walked right up to Herbie and yelled at him. I'm not proud of it, but I felt like my future depended on this race. If I won Trip's car, not only would I have a sweet, super-fast auto, but my dad would have to recognize what a skilled driver I was. I wasn't even thinking about the money anymore. Herbie and I had to win so that I would have a shot at doing what I wanted to do!

Some die-hard Herbie fans!

Charisma was home from Paris, so she came to the big event.

Even Dad, Ray, and Sally were there. They were meeting with the Bass Pro people to try to convince them to keep sponsoring Team Peyton.

Well, to make a long story short, we lost. Herbie just stopped right before the finish line! I think he was mad that I agreed to give him up if we lost. Then Trip made me take my helmet off in front of everybody.

The secret was out. "Maxx" was really Maggie Peyton. Dad was furious and my life was over.

Trip tows Herbie away. One of the worst moments of my life.

Save Herbie!

I knew right away that betting Herbie had been a huge mistake. I had to get him back. Then Charisma and I found out what Trip had done with him. He had sold him off to Jimmy D's Smash & Bash Demolition Derby! I could have killed Trip. If Herbie had to go up against all those huge monster trucks, he was going to be toast!

Herbie was right in the middle of the ring with bull's-eyes painted on him! The crowd kept chanting, "Ten cars enter! One car leaves!"

I had to save Herbie! Especially when I saw that this thing was after him!

Go Herbie!

Herbie trusted me again, but he was in bad shape when I got him back to Kevin's.

Kevin was already mad at me for letting Herbie go in the first place, but when he saw the car, he really flipped out.

I had messed up everything.

Luckily, Kevin forgave me. Now all we had to do was figure out how to repair Herbie. Again!

NASCAR NEXTEL Cup Series Qualifying Day

The next day, Ray was supposed to qualify for the NASCAR NEXTEL Cup Series race. His time would determine whether or not he would even get to participate in the race. If Ray didn't qualify, Bass Pro Shops would pull its sponsorship of Team Peyton, and it would all be over. Grandpa's dreams, Dad's dreams, my dreams—they would all go up in smoke. No pressure on Ray there. None at all!

Ray chills out before his qualifying race.

Kevin and I watch from the stands as Ray qualifies with his best time ever!

Unfortunately, right after he hit the finish line Ray spun out and ended up in the hospital!

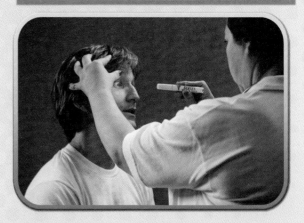

He was okay, but the doctor said he wouldn't be able to drive. Team Peyton's chances were finished. Unless . . .

NASCAR FLAGS

Ever watch a NASCAR race and wonder what the flags are all about? Here's a little rundown of the basics.

 Green: This flag is waved at the beginning of a race and at restarts. It means the track is ready to go and in safe condition. Hit the gas, baby!

 Yellow: Just like a yellow traffic light, the yellow flag means "use caution." Usually it means there's something messing up the track like an oil spill or some debris from an accident.

 Red: This flag is waved when there's a serious problem on the track, like a big accident that's blocking everyone. Drivers have to stop at a prechosen location and wait until everything's good to go.

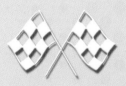 White: The white flag comes out when there's one lap left in the race.

 Black-and-white checkered: The checkered flag waves when the race has been completed. If you're over the line first when this flag is waved, you're the winner!

My First NASCAR NEXTEL Cup Series Race!

You guessed it! I stepped in as Team Peyton's new driver! I was the best driver we had and our only chance of getting Team Peyton back on track. Dad didn't know anything about it. As far as he knew, once Ray got the doctor's diagnosis, Team Peyton was out of the race. He was back home watching TV, probably trying to figure out what to do next. It was a good thing that he wasn't around, though. He definitely would have tried to stop me from racing, and I wasn't going to let anything get in my way.

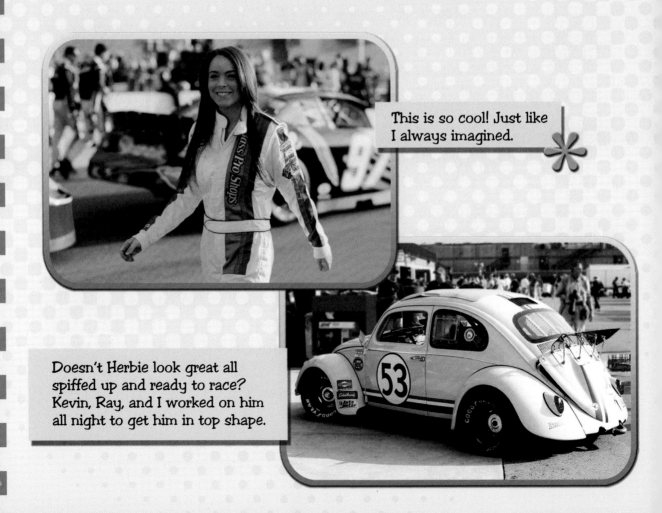

This is so cool! Just like I always imagined.

Doesn't Herbie look great all spiffed up and ready to race? Kevin, Ray, and I worked on him all night to get him in top shape.

Look at all those people! I wasn't nervous or anything. . . .

My pit crew. I had my very own pit crew!

Lookin' good, boys!

When Dad saw me racing on TV, he broke a few speed limits himself, getting to the racetrack!

Kevin talked me through the whole race. He's the best!

My pit crew in action!

Trip Murphy tried to block me out toward the end, but guess what . . .

We won!

My Dad, Ray, Sally, Kevin, and all of Team Peyton rushed to congratulate me!

Trip wasn't all that happy. But who cared?

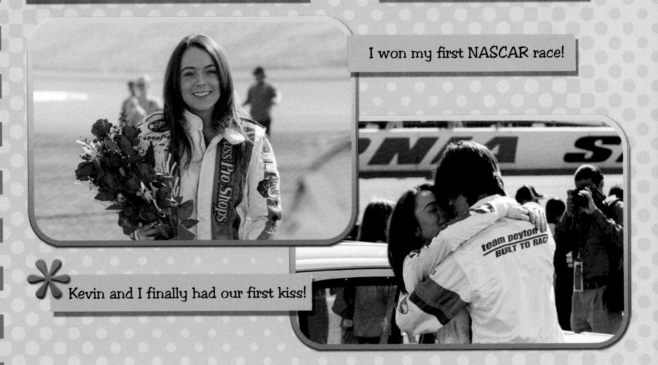

I won my first NASCAR race!

Kevin and I finally had our first kiss!

Even Dad and Sally looked cozier than ever. And Ray finally told Dad that he wanted to be a rock star.

Everything had turned out great.

Maggie Peyton's Top-Ten Tips for Winning at NASCAR

1. Don't be nervous. But if you have to be nervous, channel it into adrenaline.
2. Remember to accelerate. (I almost forgot that part.)
3. Keep your hands on the wheel at 10 and 2 o'clock.
4. Always check all your mirrors before passing.
5. Have a good pit crew to cheer you on. Family and friends are a must.
6. If you're driving a rare car, make sure you have spare parts on hand.
7. Never let another driver block you out.
8. If there's a crazy person driving next to you, you know, someone who hates you and your ride, pass him as quickly as possible.
9. It's good to have a car that can pop wheelies, flip over, rail slide, and drive on two wheels.
10. Don't crash.

And of course, LOVE YOUR CAR!

Meet The Stars!

Lindsay Lohan as Maggie Peyton

Lindsay is one of the hottest young actresses in Hollywood today, and she's also taking the music world by storm. She was born in New York on July 2, 1986, and started modeling and acting in commercials when she was just a toddler. She landed her first television role in 1996, playing Alexandra Fowler on the daytime soap, **Another World**. Movie roles were soon to follow and in 1997, Lindsay was cast as twins Hallie Parker and Annie James in Disney's remake of its classic hit, **The Parent Trap**. Lindsay's career took off after that as she landed starring roles in movies like **Freaky Friday**, **Confessions of a Teenage Drama Queen**, and **Mean Girls**. She even won an MTV Movie Award in 2004, taking home the prize for Female Breakout Star. In December 2004, Lindsay broke out in a whole new way, with her debut album, **Speak**.

Michael Keaton as Ray Peyton, Sr.

Since his first television series in 1977, Michael has done everything from comedy to drama to action. A Pennsylvania native, Michael's first big Hollywood film was *Night Shift* in 1982. He went on to star in a number of box office hits, including *Mr. Mom*, *Beetlejuice*, and *Batman*. Most recently Michael starred in the hit feature-film thriller *White Noise*.

Breckin Meyer as Ray Peyton, Jr.

Breckin has been cracking us up for years, playing both starring roles and funny bit parts in all kinds of comedies. He was born in 1974 in Minneapolis, Minnesota, before moving to California, where he attended school. Breckin has played in several homespun bands over the years (he really does play the drums), but his big claim to fame is his movie career. Breckin has appeared in such comedy classics as *Clueless*, *Can't Hardly Wait*, *Road Trip*, *Rat Race*, and *Garfield: The Movie*.

Justin Long as Kevin Meltzer

Known for his comedic timing and lovable charm, Justin is a rising star in Hollywood. He was born in Fairfield, Connecticut, and graduated from Vassar College. His first big role was on the prime-time TV show *Ed*, where he played the geeky high school student, Warren Cheswick. His first feature-film role was in *Galaxy Quest* (1999) as Brandon Wheeger. Since then, Justin has gone on to star in thrillers such as *Jeepers Creepers* in 2000, dramas such as *Crossroads* in 2002, and comedies such as *Dodgeball: A True Underdog Story* in 2004.

Matt Dillon as Trip Murphy

Born in 1964 in New Rochelle, New York, Matt first broke into the Hollywood scene in the 1980s with hit teen movies like *My Bodyguard* and *The Outsiders*. He went on to appear in over forty films, including the monster hit of 1998, *There's Something About Mary*, for which he won both a Blockbuster Entertainment Award and an MTV Movie Award.

BEHIND THE SCENES

It takes a lot of work and a little Disney magic to make Herbie come to life. When it looks like Herbie is running around on his own, there's really a team of technicians controlling him with remotes—just like one of those toy remote-control cars! (Only much, much bigger.) Plus, there isn't just one Herbie. He gets raced and beaten up and crashed and repaired so much, the filmmakers have to have a lot of Herbies on hand. Check it out!

The men behind Herbie.

Herbie's remote controls.

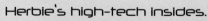

A whole lotta Herbies!

Herbie's high-tech insides.

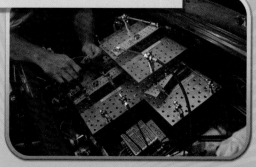

Herbie and Lindsay get ready for their close-up.

NASCAR Rocks!

Herbie Fully Loaded wouldn't have been the same without the help of these NASCAR drivers and personalities, all of whom filmed cameos playing themselves. They made Maggie and Herbie's big race authentic, and added a little racetrack humor as well.

Jeff Gordon (No. 24 DuPont Chevrolet): Jeff is a four-time NASCAR NEXTEL Cup Series Champion and has 70 career victories. He finished third in the 2004 Chase for the NASCAR NEXTEL Cup.

Kevin Harvick (No. 29 GM Goodwrench Chevrolet): Kevin was the NASCAR NEXTEL Cup Series Rookie of the Year in 2001 and also won the NASCAR Busch Series Championship that same year. In 2004 Kevin finished 14th in the NASCAR NEXTEL Cup Series.

Dale Jarrett (No. 88 UPS Ford): Dale was the NASCAR NEXTEL Cup Series Champion of 1999 and has 32 career victories.

Jimmie Johnson (No. 48 Lowe's Chevrolet): Jimmie finished second in points in 2003 and 2004 and has 14 career victories in three NASCAR NEXTEL Cup Series Seasons.

Jamie McMurray (No. 42 Texaco/Havoline Dodge): Jamie was Rookie of the Year for the 2003 season and finished 11th in points in 2004.

Casey Mears (No. 41 Target Dodge): Casey first competed in the NASCAR NEXTEL Cup Series in 2003 and finished in 35th place for the season. In 2004, he moved up to 22nd place in points.

Rusty Wallace (No. 2 Miller Lite Dodge): Rusty was the NASCAR NEXTEL Cup Series Rookie of the Year in 1984. In 1989, he was the NASCAR NEXTEL Cup Series Champion. He has 55 NASCAR NEXTEL Cup Series victories.

Richard Childress: Richard Childress Racing owns the race cars driven by Kevin Harvick, Jeff Burton and Dave Blaney. RCR cars have won over 110 NASCAR races and captured nine NASCAR series championships, including six with the late Dale Earnhardt. Richard was the first owner to win season titles in each of NASCAR's elite series—NASCAR NEXTEL Cup Series, NASCAR Busch Series, and NASCAR Craftsman Truck Series.

Benny Parsons and Allen Bestwick: These NASCAR play-by-play announcers also cameo in the film. Benny is a former NASCAR NEXTEL Cup Series champion, and Allen is a career sports reporter and anchor.

Casey Mears and Kevin Harvick on the set.

Do You Know Your Herbie History?

Before **Herbie Fully Loaded**, there were four other feature films starring Herbie. Here's a little recap of Herbie's earlier adventures.

The Love Bug [1969]

This, the original Herbie movie, was the highest grossing film of 1969. It stars Dean Jones as Jim Douglas, the hapless race car driver who is followed home by Herbie. Jones enters Herbie in a few big races, and Herbie wheels his way to victory.

Herbie Rides Again [1974]

In the second Herbie film, our adorable Volkswagen Beetle helps a woman, played by Helen Hayes, who's about to lose her house. Herbie saves the day, of course, stopping the ruthless businessmen who want to throw her out so they can build a skyscraper on her land.

Herbie Goes to Monte Carlo [1977]

In this installment, Herbie joins a race that runs from Paris to Monte Carlo. Dean Jones is back as Herbie's driver, Jim, who doesn't know that a bunch of thieves have hidden a famous stolen diamond in Herbie's gas tank. Herbie not only has to win the race, but shake the thieves that are chasing him as well.

Herbie Goes Bananas [1980]

In this film, Herbie heads to South America where he helps his new owners, played by Stephen W. Burns and Charles Martin Smith, break up a counterfeiting ring. He also takes on a pickpocket and a raging bull. Talk about some misadventures!